The Sleepover Club

Have you been invited to all these sleepovers?

Sleepover Girls
in the Ring

by Fiona Cummings

Collins
An imprint of HarperCollinsPublishers

The Sleepover Club ® is a
registered trademark of HarperCollins*Publishers* Ltd

First published in Great Britain by Collins in 2000
Collins is an imprint of HarperCollins*Publishers* Ltd
77-85 Fulham Palace Road, Hammersmith,
London, W6 8JB

The HarperCollins website address is
www.**fire**and**water**.com

3 5 7 9 8 6 4 2

Text copyright © Fiona Cummings 2000

Original series characters, plotlines
and settings © Rose Impey 1997

ISBN 0 00675500 3

The author asserts the moral right to
be identified as the author of the work.

Printed and bound in Great Britain by
Omnia Books Limited,
Glasgow

Sleepover Kit List

1. Sleeping bag
2. Pillow
3. Pyjamas or a nightdress
4. Slippers
5. Toothbrush, toothpaste, soap etc
6. Towel
7. Teddy
8. A creepy story
9. Food for a midnight feast:
   chocolate, crisps, sweets, biscuits.
   In fact anything you like to eat.
10. Torch
11. Hairbrush
12. Hair things like a bobble or hairband,
    if you need them
13. Clean knickers and socks
14. Change of clothes for the next day
15. Sleepover diary and membership card

CHAPTER ONE

Hiya! I haven't seen you for a while. We've been having a pretty wild time lately – that's why we haven't been around much. Guess where we've been? Go on! It's tough, you'll never get it. Do you give up? OK then, I'll tell you! We've only been in a circus, *that's* where. I knew you'd be amazed! The whole thing's amazed us, I can tell you. Not to mention our parents – although I don't really want to talk about that right now, it's too depressing. Because if they get their way, the Sleepover Club is finally finished – curtain down, *finito*!

Now you're looking miserable too, and we can't have that. If I tell you what we've been up to, it's bound to cheer you up. But if you hear anyone calling out "Kenny!" in a bellyaching kind of voice, just ignore them. It'll be Molly my stupid sister, and I've just about had enough of her. If it wasn't for her, our parents wouldn't be so mad with us now.

Anyway, I'm on my way to meet the others to decide how to get round our parents. I mean, we've been in messes before, as you well know, but nothing like this. This time it's BA-AD!

How did it all start? I hear you ask. Well, I'll tell you.

Right next to our school, there's this piece of open land. People hold car-boot sales on it and stuff like that. But generally it's empty, and kids just use it as a cut-through to school.

Well, one week there was *loads* of activity there. First they sealed it off so no-one could walk across it. Then loads of men in wellies appeared, making notes on clip-boards. After that, different men started marking things out on the ground. Fliss got all squeamish when she saw that and swore they were drawing around dead bodies! Then finally one day, a whole load of lorries appeared and started putting up all these really big metal poles.

"They must be building something," remarked Rosie as we were walking home.

"They look like enormous tent poles to me!" Lyndz chipped in.

"Yeah, right!" I chortled. "Like anyone would just go and put up an enormous tent right next to school."

But do you know what? That's exactly what someone *did* do. It was there in all its glory when I walked to school the next morning. And by the time we left school in the afternoon, the land was full of caravans and cars and there seemed to be hundreds of people milling about.

"I know what it is!" shrieked Fliss when she saw all the activity. "It's going to be a *circus*!"

"Cool!"

"Wicked!"

The rest of us were *really* excited, but Lyndz went all sniffy and frosty.

"It's not cool having animals cooped up in cages just so they can come out and perform for ten minutes a night," she said. "It's cruel and unkind."

Now I don't know about you, but I was amazed to hear Lyndz say that. I mean, we all know how mad Lyndz is about horses, don't we? I thought she'd *love* to see them with plumes and everything, prancing about in a circus.

Fliss must have been thinking the same thing, because she piped up, "I thought you *liked* seeing animals, Lyndz."

"Not when they're caged up with no freedom, I don't," Lyndz snapped back.

We could tell that there'd be no shifting Lyndz's opinion, so the rest of us just exchanged glances and kept quiet. And we kept quiet every day when we passed the circus, and Lyndz tutted and sighed and said how terrible it all was. Part of me knew that she was right, of course, but part of me *really* wanted to go to the circus to see the clowns and the trapeze artists and all that other stuff.

So it was a huge relief all round when we saw the first poster advertising the circus. It announced:

CIRCUS JAMBOREE

Marvel at the stupendous skill
and breath-taking dynamism
of the performers in our

ALL-HUMAN CIRCUS!

"See that?" I prodded the poster excitedly. "It's 'all human'! That means there's not an animal in sight." I turned to Lyndz. "So now do you think you might just get the *teensiest* bit excited about there being a circus in town?"

Lyndz blushed. "I guess so," she admitted.

"Hey guys, look!" Rosie was still studying the poster and jiggling up and down with excitement. "The first performance is on Saturday next week. That's your birthday, Lyndz! Now that you approve of circuses, we could all come here to celebrate. What do you say?"

We all looked eagerly at Lyndz.

"We-e-ell," she said very slowly. "Seeing as there are no animals involved, that sounds like a great idea!"

We whooped and cheered and did high fives.

"Wicked!"

"Brilliant!"

"Sad cases!"

That last comment was our arch-rivals, the M&Ms. Emily Berryman and Emma Hughes are these dweeby girls in our class who always try to spoil our fun, but there was no *way* that anyone was going to spoil our excitement today. We just pulled faces at them until they'd disappeared out of sight.

Before we split up to go our separate ways, Lyndz said, "Remember to ask whether you can come to the circus next week."

"Will we be having a sleepover afterwards too?" Rosie asked expectantly.

The smile disappeared from Lyndz's face and she shook her head. "Na-ah. Dad's doing some work on the side of the house, so there's a great gaping hole in one of the walls and part of the roof's off. Mum doesn't want the responsibility of anyone coming and injuring themselves. Sorry!"

To tell you the truth, that kind of put a damper on things. We *always* have a sleepover to celebrate our birthdays. But we didn't want to go on about it too much because Lyndz looked dead upset.

"Never mind. We'll have a great time at the circus, won't we?" giggled Frankie, pretending she was a clown juggling with imaginary balls.

"What are you doing?" I ribbed her. "You look like a performing seal, and there aren't any of those in this circus, remember?"

She whacked me on the back and, laughing, we all went our separate ways.

When I got home I was dying to tell Mum

all about the circus, but Molly was already there, boring her to death about something Edward stupid Marsh had done.

You remember my brain-dead sister, don't you? And how she has absolutely *nothing* interesting going on in her life? Well, now she spends all her time talking about this new boy in her class. He's called Edward Marsh, and we hear his stupid name about a million times a day. "Edward Marsh said this..." "Edward Marsh did that...". Bo-ring! To listen to Molly you'd think he was some kind of god.

Anyway, when I did manage to get a word in, I told Mum all about Circus Jamboree. But before Mum could say anything, Molly piped up:

"Edward Marsh told me about that. He said it's supposed to be really brilliant."

"Bully for Edward Marsh," I spat back. "If he's so wonderful I'm surprised he's not *starring* in the circus. All by himself. He could manage that, couldn't he?"

"Well actually, he's—"

I groaned. I didn't want to listen to any

more about Edward Marsh, so I yelled over the top of her: "Mum! Is it OK if I go to the circus next Saturday for Lyndz's birthday?"

That shut Molly up. She went all quiet and flounced out of the room. I called out after her:

"Ha-ha! I'm going to the circus and you're not!"

I heard her stomp upstairs and slam our bedroom door. Yeah! One-nil!

The next morning we all met up by the poster advertising the circus.

"Well?" Lyndz asked eagerly. "Mum and Dad said they'd take us. Can you come?"

We all started chattering at once, and it took a while before we realised that everyone was up for it.

"And I've got even *more* news!" announced Fliss dramatically. "Mum says that we can celebrate Lyndz's birthday at my house!"

"You mean a sleepover? Brill!"

We all started leaping about.

"Er wait, no!" Fliss squeaked. We all looked at her. "What Mum said was that we can have a birthday tea for Lyndz at my place on Sunday afternoon."

"Oh!"

It was impossible to hide our disappointment, but Lyndz recovered the quickest.

"That's great Fliss, really kind!" she smiled. "It means my birthday's going to last all weekend. How cool is that?"

We all laughed, but we knew that no *way* was tea at Fliss's going to be as much fun as a sleepover. I mean, for one thing, Fliss's mum virtually dusts us down as soon as we get through the door. It kind of takes all the pleasure out of things, if you know what I mean. And now that she's pregnant, she's probably even worse. (Yup – with *twins*, would you believe? But that, I guess, is another story.) Still, tea at her place was better than nothing.

We somehow managed to get through the week before the circus, and by the time Saturday came round I was dead excited. I put on my clean Leicester City football shirt and my best pair of jeans and went downstairs to wait for Lyndz. Her parents have this great big van, so they were collecting us all on the way to the circus. Molly was downstairs too, looking anxiously out of the window.

"Don't tell me. You're going to rush out and tell Lyndz that I'm ill and that you're going to take my place instead!" I teased.

"I'm going out too, if you must know!" she said smugly.

Actually, she *was* done up like a dog's dinner: new skirt, best shoes, loads of make-up.

"You're not going to be sad and wander about hoping that Edward Marsh will actually notice you, are you?" I chortled.

"Shut *up*, Kenny!" Molly thumped me hard on the back.

I would have flattened her, I swear, but I heard the van pull up and saw Lyndz running to the door.

The circus Big Top was amazing when we got there. I mean, it looked quite small from the outside, but when we got in and found our seats it seemed ENORMOUS. It smelt a bit damp and earthy, but it felt surprisingly warm.

"Look how high those trapezes are!" marvelled Frankie, pointing way up towards the roof of the tent. "And there isn't a safety net either!"

Shivers spread down my spine. I love doing daredevil things, but that looked a bit too scary, even for me. Fliss said she felt sick just looking up there.

More and more people crowded in until the tent was packed. Then there was a drum roll and a spotlight shone into the centre of the ring. A tall figure in a fancy red suit ran into it and introduced himself as the Ringmaster of Circus Jamboree. He told us a bit about what we'd be seeing – then it was on with the show!

I can't really begin to describe everything to you, there was too much to take in all at once. There were these amazing contortionists who actually *sat on their own heads*! And whilst they were performing, there were also acrobats doing flick-flacks and cartwheels, not just by themselves but in sort of formation. If they'd got their timing wrong, well – I don't even want to *think* about how badly they'd have been injured. And there were jugglers who juggled with everything from chairs to balls of fire. *Amazing!* And that was only in the first half! By the time the Ringmaster announced that there was going to be an interval, I felt totally exhausted!

"Isn't it brilliant!" gasped Rosie. "I didn't know where to look next!"

"And did you notice that there are three performers who look about our age?" asked Fliss. "Fancy being able to do all that! It was just unbelievable!"

"Are you enjoying it, girls?" asked Lyndz's mum. "Anyone fancy an ice-cream? I think there's someone selling them over there."

Frankie nudged me. "That's not... no, it can't be!" she said.

"Who?"

"I thought I saw Molly, that's all."

"WHAT? WHERE?"

She pointed. Just in front of the woman selling ice-creams, there did appear to be someone who looked suspiciously like Molly. And she was sitting with a couple of girls I recognised from her class.

"Come on!" I urged Frankie, and I started picking my way through the crowds towards them.

"Are you going to have a word with her?" asked Frankie, following me.

"Yeah, you could say that!" I smirked.

I'd had this *great* plan. I was going to embarrass her in front of the whole circus, and particularly in front of her stupid mates. It was obvious that Molly still hadn't spotted me, so I got down on all fours and crawled along the empty row of seats at the back of her. And as I crawled, I planned what to do. Making her jump wouldn't be enough. I'd have to do something really loud to attract the maximum attention.

Then it hit me. What is Molly always boring us at home with? You've guessed it. When I was immediately behind her I stood up and yelled at the top of my voice:

"EDWARD MARSH!"

The whole place went silent. Then a voice piped up.

"Yes! Who wants me?"

CHAPTER TWO

Well, you could have knocked me down with a feather. I hadn't actually *expected* Edward Marsh to be there, I'd just wanted to embarrass Molly by shouting out his name!!

Someone tapped me on the shoulder.

"I said, who wants me?" the same boy's voice addressed me coolly.

I turned round – and found my face covered in ice-cream.

"Oh, I'm sorry," smirked this blond creep of a boy, holding a more than slightly splodged cone. "It must have slipped!"

Molly was sitting back on her seat again and

was spluttering with laughter. "Ignore my stupid sister, Edward," she said, flashing a creepy smile at the boy. "She must have a personality disorder!"

"At least I've got a personality!" I snarled back, wiping ice-cream off my cheeks.

"Who was that boy?" squealed Fliss when we came back again. "Babe or what? Er, Kenny – did you know you had ice-cream on your face?"

That was the last thing I needed, everybody thinking Molly had got some dreamboat boyfriend.

"He's a moron!" I snapped. "Just like my stupid sister."

I was seething inside, and my face was still sticky from the ice-cream. I wished I'd never come to this stupid circus in the first place.

I held that thought for precisely thirty seconds, because once the performers started doing their stuff again, I was totally entranced. There were people spinning plates and people on stilts and people who combined the two. There were unicyclists who went up and down ramps, and one who even rode on the tightrope!

But the most amazing were the trapeze artists. They were so elegant and graceful, but all the time you knew that one false move and they could be dead. We all cheered like mad when they came down and took their bow, even Fliss, and she hadn't seen any of their act because she'd had her hands in front of her eyes all the time.

But I think my favourite act was the clowns. They were just *sooo* funny. We all still had tears streaming down our faces as we were driving home.

"That was the best birthday ever!" grinned Lyndz.

"No kidding!" I agreed. "It's going to take some beating!"

"Well don't forget you've the tea party to look forward to tomorrow!" Fliss chimed in.

The rest of us looked at each other.

"How much excitement can we handle?" Frankie mumbled under her breath.

*   *   *

I was home before Molly, because apparently Edward precious Marsh's parents had taken Molly and the other girls out for a pizza.

I was asleep before Molly came in, and I got up before she did in the morning so I didn't have to go over the whole Edward Marsh at the circus thing. Although I was *sure* that she would have told Mum and Dad all about it anyway.

It seemed ages to wait until going to Fliss's for tea, so I decided to practise a few circus skills. I mean, juggling a few balls couldn't be that difficult, surely? Well, let me tell you, it's a *lot* more difficult than it looks. I started messing about with two tennis balls, just throwing them from hand to hand. Easy-peasy. Then I tried to add a third. It was impossible. I dropped them, I threw them all at the same time, I just couldn't get the hang of it at all. I was getting really frustrated by the time Mum called me in for lunch.

"You'd better not eat too much if Nikky's put on a spread for tea," Mum told me.

"Are you kidding?" I scoffed. "Fliss's mum will have made a few sandwiches cut into pretty little shapes and some fairy cakes. I wouldn't even feel full if I ate everything she put out on the table!"

"Let's hope there's ice-cream, though," said Dad dryly. "You like ice-cream, don't you Laura?"

Mum, Dad, Molly and my older sister Emma all started to laugh. I don't know what I was madder about – the others making fun of me or Dad using my horrible name. At least they weren't going to give me a lecture about my behaviour though, which was a result.

"Just try to behave this afternoon, Kenny," Mum said firmly as she dropped me at Fliss's. "Nikky's a bit delicate now that she's pregnant, and you know what happens when she gets upset."

Yeah, she goes into a five-star tizz, that's what – and we didn't want that at all. Especially as she's expecting twins. She might go into a *ten*-star tizz!

So there I was on my best behaviour, and everything seemed to be going well. We all managed to smile and be polite, even when

Fliss's mum made us take off our shoes the minute we walked through the door. We even grinned and entered into the party spirit when she made us play silly children's games like we were three or something. I mean, it was *dead* embarrassing sitting there playing Pass the Parcel and Musical Statues. And you couldn't really tell whether Fliss's mum was having a laugh or whether she was practising for future birthday parties with the little baby twins. I wasn't wrong about the tea either.

"Another little sandwich, Kenny?" Fliss's mum asked, fluttering in front of me with a plate. "Or how about a fairy cake?"

What I really fancied was a jam doughnut, and I'd seen a plate of them on the side. Fliss's mum must have read my mind because she went to pick up the plate. But then she put it down again.

"No, I think these might be too much after all that other food. We don't want you being sick, do we?" She gave a little giggle. "Now, are you going to go and play quietly to let your tea settle? No running about, please."

We all trooped out of the kitchen and into the lounge.

"Will the fun never start?" I whispered in Frankie's ear.

"Right, what should we do?" said Fliss.

We all sat on the floor in a circle.

"I bet those kids in the circus aren't just sitting around now," I said wistfully. "I bet they're walking the tightrope or something."

"Yeah, wasn't that cool!" Frankie agreed. "Wouldn't it be ace to be able to do something like that? You could impress people wherever you went!"

We were in full discussion about the circus when Fliss's mum popped her head round the door. She beamed when she saw us sitting down. She probably thought we were playing 'ring-a-ring-a-rosies' or something.

"I'm just going upstairs to change the beds. Andy and Callum should be back from the park soon. You will be all right, won't you?"

"Yes Mum!" Fliss sighed. "I think we'll manage."

Her mum pulled a face, then closed the door behind her.

"We could always practise a few circus skills," I suggested.

Fliss looked horrified.

"I don't mean tightrope-walking or plate-spinning with your mum's best china, you idiot!" I said hastily. "What about juggling, or acrobatics? They're nice and quiet, aren't they?"

Fliss still didn't look too sure.

"We'll be dead quiet, honestly," I reassured her. "Your mum will never know."

"Has she got any wool or anything?" suggested Frankie. "We could practise juggling with that and it'll be silent if we drop it."

Fliss went upstairs to look for some wool, and the rest of us crept about downstairs. I went into the kitchen, and what should I see first? Yep, the jam doughnuts. My first thought was that I could sneak one to eat – but then I had a *brainwave*! They were ball-shaped, weren't they? Perfect for juggling! And they didn't have *that* much sugar on them, so they wouldn't make too much mess if we dropped them. And we could scoff them down before Fliss's mum reappeared. I mean, she'd obviously bought them for us to eat anyway. Sorted!

I took them back into the lounge, and Rosie appeared with a couple of those plastic plates you take on picnics, a broom and a mop.

"I thought I could practise plate-spinning with these," she explained. "They won't break when they fall. Good, eh?"

In the middle of the room, Frankie was trying to walk on her hands, with Lyndz holding her feet.

"'S not as easy as it looks, y'know," she said in an upside-down garbled voice.

"This is great!" I laughed, taking hold of the doughnuts. "It beats those poxy kids' games any day of the week!"

I tossed one of the doughnuts into the air a couple of times. Easy-peasy. A bit of sugar sprinkled on to the carpet, but nothing major. I picked up another one and started to throw that as well. When I was comfortable with that, I grabbed the third one and tried to juggle with that too. A doughnut fell to the floor. I tried again. One landed on the sofa.

"OK Kenny, you can do this!" I told myself.

I grabbed the doughnuts and slowly, slowly threw them into the air. And do you know what? *I actually started to juggle with them*. I couldn't believe it!

"Hey guys, look at me!" I yelled.

Lyndz stopped to watch, and let go of Frankie's legs. THUD! Franks tumbled on to the carpet. That kind of made me lose my concentration, so I bumped into Rosie and dropped one of the doughnuts. Which wouldn't have been so bad if Fliss hadn't chosen just that moment to come through the door.

"Whaddayadoing?" she shrieked. Then – *SQUELCH*. She trod on the doughnut.

Well, you would not *believe* the amount of jam that spurted out of it and shot across the carpet in a red streak. I mean, when you eat a doughnut there never seems to be that much jam in the middle, does there?

Fliss kind of yelped, then went white.

"Mum's going to *kill* us!" she squealed.

"It's not that bad," I reassured her, and scooped up the jam with my finger.

Unfortunately, the trail of jam now looked worse than ever against the cream carpet.

"I think I can hear someone coming!" hissed Rosie.

I quickly grabbed the other two doughnuts, shoved one in my mouth and the other in the back pocket of my jeans.

"Baaborginagaig!" I commanded, although my mouth was so stuffed with doughnut I couldn't make myself understood.

The others looked at me blankly. I got down on the floor and did a handstand to show them what I meant, balancing over the jammy stain so that if Fliss's mum did come in she wouldn't see it.

"Gotcha! You mean you want us to carry on doing handstands and stuff, don't you?" Frankie grasped at last. "Well, why didn't you just say so?"

But I was upside down with a mouthful of doughnut, wasn't I? Not a great place to be in, all in all... I started to splutter, I started to cough, then I started to choke.

"Are you OK, Kenny?" Rosie asked. "You don't look too good!"

"Come on Kenny, deep breaths!" Lyndz slapped me hard on the back.

I gasped and coughed and the remains of the doughnut sprayed out all over the lounge – and all over Fliss's mum, who had come in to see what all the noise was about.

It was hard to tell what her first reaction was going to be. She went kind of red, then very, *very* white. I thought she was going to cry, or maybe collapse with shock. But none of us was prepared for the ear-splitting shriek that eventually burst from her lips.

"GET OUT OF MY HOUSE! N-O-O-O-W-W!"

Well, we weren't going to argue with that! We left the house running, grabbing any old shoes on the way out of the door. We ran down the path and on to the pavement, only stopping when we were well out of sight. Gasping, we exchanged shoes so that somehow we ended up with the right pairs.

"Poor Fliss!" said Frankie at last. "Do you

think she's going to be all right?"

"I hope so," I murmured.

But I think we all knew then that "The Jam Doughnut Incident" was going to have *serious* consequences for the Sleepover Club.

CHAPTER THREE

It was pretty obvious to my parents that something was wrong when I arrived home from Fliss's so early. Plus, Dad was already standing in the hall holding the phone receiver about a mile from his ear. I could hear someone screaming and yelling on the other end. No prizes for guessing who *that* was! Mum reluctantly took the receiver from Dad and leant against the hall table.

"Hello Nikky, it's Valerie. I think you'd better start from the beginning."

The sobs from the other end of the phone quietened a little, and Mum went into her patient-listening mode. I crept up the stairs and sat down near the top. I kind of wanted to know what Fliss's mum was saying, but I daren't really go any closer.

After what felt like about six hours, Mum finally put the phone down and had a muted conversation with Dad. Then she called upstairs angrily:

"Laura McKenzie! Get yourself down here, *now*!"

Oh-oh. This wasn't good. This wasn't good at all.

As I walked into the lounge, Molly shuffled out, smirking.

"You're for it now, dog-breath!" she goaded.

I didn't even feel like punching her.

"Sit down!" Both my parents had their "this-is-very-serious" expressions on.

"That was Fliss's mum on the phone," Mum began, like I couldn't guess that for myself. "She is very upset..." BLAH BLAH BLAH... "we're very disappointed in you..." BLAH BLAH BLAH... "thought we could trust you but you're obviously still acting like a toddler…"

Yeah right, like a toddler would be able to juggle with doughnuts, I *don't* think!

"… Fliss's mum feels, and I have to say that in this case we agree with her, that there should be no more sleepovers, no more socialising with the others at *all*, until you all prove that you can behave more responsibly."

"WHAT?" I gasped.

"And if Fliss's mum had her way," Dad said very calmly, "you wouldn't be allowed to even *talk* to each other, so think yourself very lucky, my girl!"

"I just cannot believe that you would upset Fliss's mum like that when you know that she's pregnant and should be taking things a bit easier." Mum looked at me *reeeally* reproachfully.

This was seriously serious. It was like Leicester City losing 6-0 in the FA Cup Final and me getting beaten up by Molly all rolled into one. I slunk upstairs and climbed on to my bed. I was so miserable, I didn't even notice that my stomach was rumbling with hunger.

"You sound like a clogged-up drainpipe!" moaned Molly, who was sprawled out on her bed.

"Shut your face!" I snapped, and turned over so my back was towards her. She started to say something else, but I stuffed my pillow over my ears so I couldn't hear her. I wasn't even in the mood for a fight, so you can tell how miserable I felt.

The next morning I still felt bad. Worse, even. I would have to face the others, and they were bound to say it was all my fault. They always say that when our parents give us grief about anything. I mean, I can't help it if my brain comes up with all these great ideas, can I? Frankie and the others are always happy enough to join in at the time. It's only when we get parent problems that they start to complain. And Fliss's mum is one HUGE problem when it comes to us having fun, even when she's *not* pregnant.

"Looks like you had as bad a night as we

did!" Rosie mumbled when I joined her and the others in the playground. They were all there apart from Fliss. And when Fliss arrived, she looked absolutely *dreadful*. Her skin is very pale at the best of times, but that morning it looked almost transparent. She had huge dark circles under her eyes and she looked like she'd been crying all night.

"Don't say anything," she whimpered. "I know Mum was out of order to go off on one like that, but she's been going on at me all night about putting her health at risk. I can't take any more." And she dissolved into racking sobs.

We all crowded round and Frankie gave her a big hug.

"I know things got a bit out of hand yesterday. Didn't they, Kenny?" Frankie looked at me menacingly. "But it wasn't *that* bad, was it? I mean we're not going to let anyone stop us seeing each other because of a jam doughnut, are we?"

"NO!" we all chorused.

Fliss just sniffed a bit.

"We've just got to play it cool for a while

and show that we're responsible and it'll all blow over. You'll see," Frankie finished.

Fliss didn't look too sure, but the rest of us grinned and nodded bravely. The bell went for the start of school, so we all walked to the classroom, feeling a bit brighter than we had done earlier.

Mrs Weaver was standing at the front with a wiry scrap of a girl. She had dark hair tied in plaits, really dark eyes, and lips which were pursed into a tight thin line. She stared at us all defiantly as we trooped in and sat down.

"Well everybody, we have a new addition in our class today," Mrs Weaver beamed at us. "This is Ailsa, and she'll be joining us for a term. I hope you'll all make her very welcome and make sure that she settles in all right."

She motioned Ailsa to sit at an empty space at the table in front of ours. Everybody turned to look at her. Well, *we* didn't, of course – we tried to play it a bit casual. We just sneaked little glances to try to suss out what she was going to be like.

All I could think was that she wouldn't be much good at football. She was too small.

"She looks a bit familiar, doesn't she?" Fliss whispered.

"I know what you mean," Rosie murmured back.

But none of us could think where we'd seen her before.

At break time when we were going to say hi, the M&Ms swept her away.

"Come with us Ailsa, we'll look after you!" smarmed Emma Hughes.

But at the end of break, Ailsa walked back into the classroom by herself. And when the M&Ms appeared, they stuck their noses in the air and did their best to avoid her.

"Well, they obviously didn't make much of an impression on Ailsa!" laughed Rosie. "She must have some taste!"

"I just wish I could think where I've seen her before," complained Fliss. "It's really bugging me."

We didn't have chance to catch up with her at lunchtime, because Miss Burnie had called an extra netball practice and for once we were all on the team. I thought I caught a glimpse of Ailsa watching us at the side of the court, but when I turned round she'd gone.

As if that wasn't enough exercise, we had a gym lesson after lunch too. Actually, that's my idea of heaven – it beats boring maths any day. But poor Fliss seemed quite exhausted.

"At least Ailsa will be able to sit it out, 'cos she won't have got any gym kit with her," Fliss said hopefully. "Maybe I can join her."

But she was wrong on both counts. Mrs Weaver insisted that Fliss took part, and Ailsa did have her kit with her. In fact, she was the first to get ready. We were all still struggling into our shorts, and there she was in a sort of leotard thing and proper gymnast's leggings.

"Just who does she think she is?" sniffed Emily Berryman as she made her way into the gym. "She looks ridiculous, if you ask me!"

But the old cogs were beginning to whir in my brain. She definitely looked very familiar.

Suddenly it came to me!

"I've got it!" I shouted excitedly to the others. "She's—"

Just then, Ailsa started to do a series of flick-flacks and cartwheels the length of the gym, ending in a super-dooper double somersault.

"Wowee!"

Everyone started to clap and cheer.

"She's from the Circus Jamboree!" Fliss and I said at the same time. "Come on! We've *got* to talk to her now!"

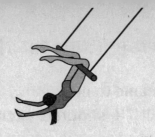

CHAPTER FOUR

"That was amazing!"

"I wish I could do that!"

"Did it take you long to learn? Can you teach us?"

"You're from Circus Jamboree, aren't you?" said Lyndz eagerly.

An agitated expression spread across Ailsa's face. Then she just stared away across the gym. We looked at each other, puzzled.

"I only wanted to say how fantastic it was!" Lyndz carried on, sheepishly. "We went for my birthday and it was the best birthday ever. It was totally brilliant!"

"Yeah! We wish we belonged to a circus!" I assured her. "It must be ace performing like that, making everyone wish they could do what you can do."

Ailsa shrugged. "It's all right." But she was kind of grinning as she said it.

"Do you think you could teach us to do what you just did?" Frankie asked again.

Ailsa eyed us up and down and started to giggle. I guess we did look kind of funny. We all have such different physiques, and none of us looks wiry like her. I mean, Fliss is kind of thin and everything, but she's not got what you might call any *muscles* to speak of. And I guess you need those if you're going to perform so many flick-flacks one after the other.

"I could try," Ailsa said thoughtfully. "But I'm not making any promises. I've been doing this all my life, remember!"

Mrs Weaver came over to us. I think she'd been dealing with Ryan Scott in the boys' changing room when Ailsa had put on her performance, so she didn't know what all the buzz in the gym was about.

"Well Ailsa, I hope Laura and her friends are showing you the ropes," she said breezily.

"Actually, we were hoping Ailsa would show *us* the ropes, Mrs Weaver," I said seriously. "The tightropes, of course!"

We all started spluttering with laughter, even Ailsa.

For the rest of the lesson we worked in a group with her. I think Mrs Weaver was just so glad that Ailsa was fitting in that she virtually left us to our own devices, which meant that we could learn the art of flick-flacks. Well, ehem, excuse me if I don't show you right now how *that* went. All you need to know is that we went home with severely bruised bums and crushed egos!

We actually walked home with Ailsa as far as the circus. She was really nice, but she didn't seem to want to talk about what it was like travelling around the country. Just before we left her, Frankie asked:

"Did the M&Ms do something to upset you at break time?"

Ailsa looked puzzled. "Excuse me? Oh you

mean Emma what's-her-face and her little friend?"

We nodded.

"Nah," said Ailsa quietly, "they were just really snotty when I told them where I lived. They said they couldn't imagine anything so awful as living in a caravan all the time."

"Well, don't you take any notice of them!" I said indignantly. "They're pond-scum, they wouldn't know a good thing if it bit them on the bum!"

After that we spent a lot of time with Ailsa. It did feel a bit strange that there were six of us hanging round together instead of five, but it was kind of cool having someone new to tell about our adventures. She seemed well impressed by some of them. And a bit sad too that she didn't have such good friends to share things with.

"I thought there were other kids in the circus," Fliss said.

"There are, but they're a bit older than me and we don't have so much in common," she explained.

"Like me and Molly the Monster,"

I groaned, and the others all pulled gruesome faces.

I hadn't told Molly about Ailsa. I suppose the fact that we weren't really speaking to each other had something to do with that. In fact, every time we saw each other we just scowled and pulled faces. Molly didn't even mention Edward stupid Marsh at mealtimes any more. But I could tell that she was excited about something, because she was always on the phone to her mates. Not that I could ever hear what she was saying, because whenever I went near her she hissed into the phone: "Scuzzball sister alert!" and shut up until I'd gone away again.

I didn't care. I had something far more exciting to think about.

One day after school, Ailsa actually invited us back to the circus with her. First she took us into the caravan where she lived with her parents. It was absolutely amazing. It wasn't like Jewel's hippy caravan at the protest site earlier this year. It wasn't like our tiny little holiday caravan, either. It was *enormous*! There seemed to be loads of room with a proper kitchen and two big bedrooms. They even had satellite TV!

Her mum was dead nice too. She apparently used to be a trapeze artist and an acrobat too.

"But I feel a bit long in the tooth for that these days!" she smiled.

"No way!" we all chorused. She looked even younger than Fliss's mum!

"Ooh Ailsa, I like your friends!" Ailsa's mum started shrieking with laughter. "They say all the right things!"

"I think Mum would really like to be a proper teacher. You know, like Mrs Weaver," Ailsa confided to us over Coke and crisps when her mum had gone outside. "She'd make a brilliant games teacher anyway. She's got loads of certificates for all the training she's done."

"Hey, she could teach us a few circus skills!" Frankie laughed. "That would be good practice for her. If she could cope with Kenny, she could cope with anyone!"

"Thanks very much!" I punched her lightly on the arm. "I think I'd be quite good on the trapeze, actually!"

Just then, a figure appeared in the doorway.

"Hiya, Dad!" Ailsa got up and gave him a hug. "These are my new friends from school."

"Hello there!" the man beamed at us. It was only when he spoke that we recognised who he was. It was the *Ringmaster*! He was dressed in jeans and a sweatshirt, and he looked kind of different from when he was all done up in his red suit.

"Well, I guess you guys would like a quick tour, would you?" he asked.

"Yes please!" we chorused.

We slurped down our drinks and followed him into the Big Top. It felt a bit weird going inside when there wasn't an audience. But there were loads of performers practising for that evening's show. Jugglers were flipping balls over our heads, unicyclists were speeding up and down ramps, and the trapeze artists were practising their moves.

"They've got a safety net!" Rosie pointed.

"They always practise with the net,"

Ailsa's father explained. "They practise new moves all the time, and it's only when they're confident that they perform them in the shows without the net."

"It still looks a long way down!" Fliss whispered. "You'd never catch me up there!"

"Oh, I'd love it!" I grinned, happily forgetting how scared I'd been watching the trapeze act on Lyndz's birthday. "In fact, I'd love to do *any* of the stuff in the circus, it all looks so cool!"

Ailsa's father smiled. "Well, cool or not, it needs lots of practice, doesn't it, Ails? And I think that's what you should be doing right now. You've got a show tonight, remember?"

Ailsa shrugged.

"Your friends can come by another time, don't worry." Her father ruffled her hair. "It's been good to meet you all," he said, turning to us. "Thanks for helping Ailsa to settle in so well here. It's kind of tough for her when we move around so much, and it's not always easy making new friends."

Ailsa was rolling her eyes and looking dead embarrassed.

"No worries," I told him. "We'll just expect Ailsa to teach us all she knows about circus skills before she leaves!"

We were still buzzing with the excitement of having been behind the scenes at the circus when Ailsa ran into school the next morning. Her cheeks were all flushed and her eyes were sparkling. The M&Ms looked at her curiously, but she just ignored them and came flying up to us.

"You... circus... half-term!" she panted.

"Huh?" We stared at her.

"Calm down!" Frankie commanded. "And tell us again – slowly!"

"You... at the circus... half-term!" Ailsa was still too excited to get her words out properly.

"You want us to come to the circus at half-term?" asked Lyndz.

Ailsa nodded.

"You mean you'll give us free tickets?" asked Rosie hopefully.

Ailsa shook her head. We all looked disappointed.

Ailsa started laughing. "No, it's better than that!" she said excitedly, having finally recovered herself. "Mum and Dad say you can come and learn circus skills with us over half-term!"

We stared at her, totally stunned.

"D'you mean it?" I whispered at last, hardly able to believe my luck. "That's brilliant!"

And we all started whooping and cheering and leaping around.

When the bell went, we kind of floated into the classroom. It was going to be SUPERB! I could see myself now, doing death-defying stunts on the trapeze and the crowd cheering wildly far below. I mean, I know that I want to become Leicester City's star striker and everything, but there was nothing stopping me having a career in the circus first!

It was Fliss who brought us back down to earth. We were in the middle of the Numeracy Hour later that day when she suddenly gasped, "Oh no!" and went very pale.

"What's up?" I hissed, but she couldn't reply because Mrs Weaver was focusing her beady eyes on us.

When it was break time, we followed Fliss into the cloakroom where she slumped down on one of the benches.

"We can't go to the circus at half-term," she mumbled very quietly. "The Jam Doughnut Incident, remember? We're not allowed to see each other outside school."

CHAPTER FIVE

The Jam Doughnut Incident! How could we have forgotten it?

"There's no *way* Mum will let me go to learn circus skills," Fliss moaned. "She'll go ballistic if I even ask her."

The rest of us looked at each other glumly.

"Our parents were pretty mad, weren't they?" we agreed.

"Look," I said firmly, trying to be upbeat. "We've got to give this our best shot. I mean, it's not every day that professionals volunteer to teach us circus skills, is it? Think positive!"

The others looked about as positive as I felt when we left each other that afternoon. I kept rehearsing in my mind how I should tell Mum about our plans for half-term. But there never seemed to be the right time to bring it up because Molly the stupid Monster was always there. And I was determined that she shouldn't find out about it. The last thing I needed was for her to mess things up for me.

You can tell how desperate I was when I actually volunteered to help with the washing-up after dinner. Everyone looked at me suspiciously, and Molly mouthed "Creep!" as I carried the plates into the kitchen.

"So Kenny, what do you want?" asked Mum, swishing the plates around in sudsy water.

"What?" I gasped, looking shocked. "Can't I help my own mum with the washing-up if I want to?"

"Well, you could, Kenny," Mum agreed. "But the only time you ever do is when you want something."

"OK, I'll come clean!" I giggled, pointing at the dirty water. Then I got serious. "Well you see, the thing is…"

I checked that Molly wasn't anywhere around and closed the door before continuing.

"Ailsa is this girl who belongs to Circus Jamboree and she's in our class for a term. We've kind of been looking after her and making sure she settles down at school. Well, yesterday we met her parents, and they said they'd like to teach us circus skills in the half-term holiday."

"Oh?" Mum raised her eyebrows. "You mean they volunteered, just like that?"

"Yes – well, no. Ailsa's mum teaches the people in the circus how to be acrobats, and we said how much we'd like to learn."

"Hmm," Mum looked doubtful. "Is it safe?"

"Oh yes!" I promised. "Ailsa's mum is fully trained, and Ailsa's dad is really hot on safety."

"Hmm," Mum said again.

"Well?" I asked. "Can I go?"

"I don't know." Mum wiped her hands on a towel. "We did agree that after that last catastrophe we were going to keep you apart for a while, didn't we?"

"But Mum—" I moaned.

"But Mum nothing," Mum said crisply. "I'm going to have to think about this."

"Well, you won't mention it to Molly, will you?" I pleaded. "I don't want her sticking her nose in."

I dragged myself upstairs and flung myself on the bed. I couldn't see what Mum's problem was. I mean, it was Fliss's mum who had blown the Jam Doughnut Incident out of all proportion. It wasn't our fault that she can be so neurotic sometimes. I consoled myself with the fact that the others must be having the same grief from their oldies. But I was wrong about that too.

When I got to school the next day, Frankie, Lyndz and Rosie were all chattering to Ailsa.

"It's going to be so great next week, isn't it Kenny?" Frankie grabbed me excitedly. "Who'd have thought we'd be learning how to juggle and stuff, in a real Big Top?"

All the air seemed to get sucked out of me,

and it took a few moments before I could find my voice.

"What? You mean you're allowed to go?" I gasped.

"Well, yes," Frankie said, sensing that something was wrong. "Izzy has colic and Mum's really tired. I think she thought it would give all of us a break if I did something with you lot during half-term."

"Oh," I mumbled. "Can you go, Lyndz?"

"Yep," Lyndz nodded, smiling. "Our house is always a bit crazy during school holidays with there being five of us at home. And when I told Mum about being able to go to the circus every day, she leapt at the idea."

"Yeah, I think my mum thought it would be cheaper if I was there rather than being at home," Rosie admitted. "She's just splashed out on new throws and rugs and stuff for the lounge, and I think she's a bit strapped for cash now. And if I'm at home, we'll only end up going shopping or ice-skating or something. So she was kind of relieved when I told her about Ailsa's parents teaching us circus skills."

"I see." My misery had just multiplied.

But at least Fliss understood how I felt. When she arrived she was almost in tears.

"Mum says there's no way I can come along to the circus next week," she sobbed. "I bet she won't even let me out of the house!"

So that meant that all the others would be having the time of their lives, and I would be stuck at home with not even Fliss to mess about with. It was *so* unfair.

At break time, Frankie pulled me aside as the others went to get their coats.

"It won't be any fun without you next week," she whispered. "You've got to get your mum to change her mind. Do you want my mum to have a word with her?"

That was the best suggestion anybody'd had for ages. I mean, Frankie's mum's a lawyer! If anyone could put up a persuasive argument for me to be allowed to learn circus skills with the others, it was her.

"It's got to be worth a try," I shrugged.

I tried to be cool about it, but all evening I was in a permanent state of panic just waiting for the phone to ring. I had a couple of false alarms when patients called wanting Dad's advice. But third time lucky. I knew it was Frankie's mum on the phone when Mum said "Hello, Helena," then didn't manage to say anything else except "yes", "no" and "I agree" for the next half an hour.

When she came off the phone I dived out of the lounge to see what she'd decided – only for her to shoo me away whilst she made another phone call. I was *desperate* to know what was going on. I mean, my happiness depended on her decision! But did she put me out of my misery? No, she did not. She was still on the phone when I went to bed. And in the morning I didn't have a chance to ask Mum either because we were in such a rush and Molly was always there.

I felt *terrible* when I got to school, especially when I saw Fliss leaping about with the others in the playground.

"Great, that's all I need," I told myself through gritted teeth. "Little Miss Prissy can go to the circus and I'm the only one who can't."

As soon as they saw me the others all came

hurtling towards me.

"Isn't it great?" they squealed.

"Marvellous!" I said sarcastically.

"Aren't you pleased that you're coming to learn circus skills too?" Ailsa looked at me, amazed. "I thought you wanted to."

"But…"

"You don't know, do you?" shrieked Fliss.

I shook my head, dazed.

"My mum rang your mum and told her that everyone was going and we'd all promised to be on our best behaviour," gabbled Frankie. "So your mum rang Fliss's mum and they both agreed that you two could come as well!"

"YESSS!" I clenched my fists in a victory salute. I was going after all!!

The following week on the Monday morning, the five of us met outside Circus Jamboree. Ailsa's father opened the gates and let us through. Then he looked up and down the road.

"You're eager beavers!" he grinned. "Come on through, we might as well wait for the others in the Big Top."

He led the way towards the circus tent.

"Others?" We looked at each other.

"He must mean the other circus performers," Rosie said. "Maybe we'll be practising with them."

The Big Top seemed even larger than when we'd last been in it. There was no-one else about, until Ailsa appeared.

"Hi there." She was looking a bit sheepish. "There's something I'd better tell you…"

"Your mum's not ill, is she? We can still learn circus skills?" I asked anxiously.

"Yes, but—"

Ailsa was interrupted by a volley of laughter. More people were entering the tent.

"The rest of the group's already here," Ailsa's father was saying breezily.

We all looked at each other. There must have been some mistake! We hadn't planned to meet anyone else. We turned round to see who had joined us – and I got the shock of my life.

"*Molly?*" I shrieked. "What are YOU doing here??"

CHAPTER SIX

I just couldn't believe my eyes. I thought at first that Molly was playing a trick on me, but you could tell from the expression on her face that she hadn't been expecting to see me either.

"So," I glared at her. "What *are* you doing here?"

"Erm, that's what I wanted to tell you." Ailsa had sidled up beside me. "The older kids from the circus found out that you lot were coming, and asked whether their new classmates could come too."

"Yeah, André invited us, ice-cream girl!"

Standing grinning before me was the loathsome Edward Marsh. I just *knew* that he had to be involved in this somewhere. Beside them was a tall, dark-haired boy with olive skin. I kind of remembered seeing him in the circus, but Molly had never mentioned that he had joined their class.

"I really do not believe this," I hissed under my breath, and went back to join my friends.

"I'm sorry," Ailsa kept saying. "I only found out that there were other people coming last night. And by then it was too late to warn you."

"It's not the other people we mind," I told her. "It's my stupid sister and her gruesome boyfriend."

"Well, maybe if you and Molly were actually *talking* to each other this might not have happened," Frankie suggested coolly.

Ailsa's father clapped his hands for our attention. He was standing with Ailsa's mum and this clown who was wearing an enormous blue wig, a shiny hat and the longest shoes you've ever seen.

"I'm the Ringmaster at Circus Jamboree," he said to everyone, "which means it's my job to keep everything running smoothly. So first I'm going to split you into two groups…"

Frankie, Lyndz, Rosie, Fliss and I grinned at each other.

"… but I thought it might be fun if we mixed you up a bit so you could make new friends."

We all looked at each other in horror!

Ailsa's dad started pointing at us. "You lot go in that group over there with my wife Carina, and the rest of you go and stand with Bobby the clown."

This whole thing was rapidly turning into a *nightmare*! Ailsa's dad had only put me in a group with Fliss, Ailsa, two other girls I didn't know and, wait for it – *Molly the big ugly Monster*. I mean, come on! There was no way I was going to spend half-term week with *her*!

It was pretty obvious that she felt the same, because she snarled as soon as she joined me. Then, when she thought no one was looking, she pinched my leg, hard. I yelped, then I pinched her back, harder. To start with, no one realised what was going on. But by the time we had progressed to thumping each other and yanking each other's hair, everybody had wised up to the fact that we really couldn't stand being in the same group.

When Ailsa's dad and Bobby the clown finally pulled us apart, Molly and I stood panting, scowling at each other. Ailsa's dad looked horrified.

"Well, I didn't realise that splitting you up would lead to the outbreak of World War Three. I think maybe we'd better stick to the groups you came in."

We all reassembled. He went on rather sharply:

"Can I just say that we don't have animals of any description in this circus, and what we just witnessed looked very much like a cat fight to me. If there's a performance like that again, I'm afraid you can *all* say goodbye to learning circus skills. Is that understood?"

We all nodded sheepishly, and I felt really

bad. I mean, Ailsa's family were putting themselves out for us here, and we'd already spoilt it. Although Molly *had* started it, of course.

Anyway, once me and Molly were away from each other, we started with the real circus stuff. But whereas I had hoped to be walking the tightrope at the very least, we were with Bobby the clown. That should have been cool, but he was making balloon elephants like we were at a kids' party or something!

"Boy, is this tame!" I whispered to Frankie. "We didn't need to come here to learn how to do that. I thought we'd be learning all the good stuff!"

Frankie ignored me, and Fliss went "Sshh!" and looked really annoyed.

I gazed over to where Ailsa's mum was teaching Molly's group. Some of them were practising walking on their hands with a partner and some were testing out some baby stilts.

"Hey, look at them!" I nudged Frankie again. "D'you think we'll be doing that soon instead of this boring stuff?"

I don't know if Bobby the clown heard me or not, but he let go of the balloon he was holding and it ended up flying right in my face, making a disgusting noise.

"Well, excu-u-use you!" he said, holding his pretend red nose and making it squeak. "You seem to have a bit of a wind problem!"

The others fell about as though it was the funniest thing they'd ever heard.

"So what's your name?" Bobby asked.

"Kenny," I replied quietly.

"Well Kenny, thank you for volunteering for this next section. Just step this way…"

I had to go and walk round the ring after him, but he walked really strangely because of his big shoes and he made me do the same. At first I felt a right dill, but soon I got into it and started goofing around after him. Suddenly he stopped.

"What's that?" he yelled, pointing to the ceiling.

I looked up and – SPLAT! He got me in the chops with a foam pie. He must have had it under his hat! The others were just about *wetting* themselves, and so was Molly's group. I was seething, but I tried not to let anyone see. I just wiped a load of foam from my face and flung it in Molly's direction. It actually landed on Edward Marsh's neat cargo pants, which was just as satisfying.

"I think Kenny deserves a big round of applause for being a good sport," Bobby encouraged the others. "One of the first rules of being a good clown is to respond to others, and Kenny did just that. Well done!"

I took a big bow and noticed that Molly wasn't clapping. She was obviously dead jealous that I'd been praised like that. Maybe it wasn't so bad that she was there after all... If she proved to be useless at circus skills, as I was sure that she would, then it would give me something to goad her about in future. And that could only be a good thing, couldn't it?

After that wobbly start, the rest of the day was *excellent*. The groups swapped over and Ailsa's mum trained us in the basics of being acrobats. Fliss was ace at walking on her hands, but Frankie was a bit of a disaster – I think her feet were too heavy and kept making her fall over. It all seemed to come so naturally to Ailsa, who kept doing flick-flacks round the ring to encourage us.

We'd all taken a packed lunch, and as we sat in the seats to eat it, the real circus performers came into the ring to practise. That was *fantastic*. The jugglers and the contortionists were there, but it was the trapeze artists who were amazing. They just swung about and did flips like it was no effort at all. Sometimes they swung across the ring on the first trapeze, then did a triple somersault or something, grabbing the second trapeze about a split second after another person had swung away from it. Whenever they finished a particular move, we all clapped and cheered. Fliss could just about bring herself to watch it because they had the safety net up.

When Ailsa's dad called us all back into our groups, he grinned. "So you'd all like to be trapeze artists, then?"

"YES!"

"Well, you know it's taken these guys years and years to learn what you've just seen. We just couldn't teach you that in a week," he explained.

We all went, "Aw!"

"But for one afternoon only, Mischa and Katya, our most experienced trapeze artists, have agreed to give all those who want one, a go on the trapeze."

"Brilliant!"

"Excellent!"

"They're lowering the trapeze for safety reasons," Ailsa's dad went on, "but I have to warn you, it still looks an awfully long way down. If you're brave, have a go. If not, and I have to tell you that you'd never get *me* up there, Sally is going to be demonstrating unicycle skills and Simon will be leading the juggling classes."

"Come on, we've got to do this!" I urged the others.

"OK," said Frankie a little nervously. "I guess we'll never get another chance."

Lyndz and Rosie both nodded their agreement.

"Well, I'm staying right here to have a go on the unicycle," Fliss told us firmly. "If it's too scary for Ailsa's dad, it's too scary for me!"

"Aw Fliss, come on, give it a go!" I encouraged her. "It'll be perfectly safe – look, they're lowering the trapeze right down. You'll kick yourself when we're all raving about how brilliant it is."

"Well that's a chance I'm prepared to take," Fliss sniffed, sounding just like her mum.

"Right, all those who want a go on the trapeze, line up here," Ailsa's dad called. "There's no need to push, everyone will get a go."

We all crowded over to the bottom of those scaffolding-like steps which trapeze artists have to climb up. I saw Molly rushing over too, so I elbowed her out of the way to make sure that I was in front of her in the queue. In fact, I elbowed *everybody* out of the way, so what do you know? I was the *first* in the queue.

Standing at the bottom of the scaffolding, it looked an awfully long way to have to climb up. Butterflies started going crazy in my stomach. I couldn't wait to have a go on the trapeze, but at the same time part of me wanted to run back and learn the unicycle with Fliss...

"OK, who's first?" Katya called down from the top.

I started climbing with legs quivering like blancmange. It seemed to go on forever! I got level with the net, and still I had to climb up further until Katya reached out a hand and pulled me on to the tiny platform with her. I looked down, and kind of wished I hadn't.

"Are you ready?" asked Katya kindly. "First, just get a feel for the trapeze."

She held it out for me, and I grabbed on to it. It felt narrower than I'd expected.

"Just swing out a few times and get the momentum going," she advised. "Then Mischa will try to catch you. Don't look down, just focus on your movement. And if you fall, just relax and make yourself all floppy – the safety net will do the rest. OK, are you ready?"

I wasn't sure, to be honest, but I nodded and took a couple of deep breaths. Then

Katya pushed me gently away from the platform – and I was flying! It was just the best feeling ever!! It was like swinging in space with nothing else around. I swung once, twice, three times, and then I saw Mischa swinging towards me, upside down.

"Next time, try and grab my hands," he shouted.

It looked kind of easy. But when I swung out again, I couldn't let go.

"Don't worry, next time!" he called as I swung away from him.

I braced myself. I could see him getting nearer and nearer. I let go, tried to grab his hand and… I was falling and falling, but I didn't seem to be getting anywhere. The net wasn't so far down, surely? I must have missed it and was falling right to the ground! I tried to scream but I couldn't. Visions of ambulances and hospitals flashed in front of me. What if I didn't make it? What if I was going to die?

BOING! I hit the net and seemed to shoot back about twenty feet into the air. Then I started to laugh and giggle. That had been the most *incredible* experience! I'd have liked to stay bouncing on the net all day, but one of the other trapeze guys came and helped me off. Someone else was waiting to go at the top and they had to make sure that the net was clear below.

My legs were shaking more when I climbed down off the scaffolding than they had when I'd climbed up it. But this time they were shaking through sheer excitement.

Fliss came rushing up to me.

"Was it good?" she demanded. "What was it like?"

"Amazing!" I panted. "Totally brilliant! You ought to do it."

"Look, Molly's having a go!" Fliss pointed up.

I'd only just looked up when Molly took hold of the trapeze, swung out half-way, then fell off.

"Way to go, Molly!" I shrieked.

Whilst some of the other kids were having a go, an ashen Molly staggered from the scaffolding.

"Oh dear, scared of heights, are we?" I sniggered. "Does Edward Marsh know what a wimp you are, then?"

"You weren't as good as Kenny, were you?" taunted Fliss. "At least she managed a few swings on it. And she only just missed the other trapeze."

Molly narrowed her eyes at Fliss. "If you're such an expert, you ought to show us all how it's done. Go on, then! Or are you just a chicken with a big mouth?"

She started to cluck. I could see Fliss getting hot and bothered and more and more agitated.

"Cluck, cluck, chicken!" Molly squawked right in Fliss's face.

"Right!" Fliss yelled eventually. "I'll show you!"

And she stalked away towards the scaffolding.

Now, you know as well as I do that Fliss just isn't good with heights, or anything the tiniest bit scary. This could mean only one thing – DISASTER!

CHAPTER SEVEN

"Come back, Fliss!" I shouted, chasing after her. "You don't have to prove anything to my stupid sister!"

Fliss turned and stared at me. She was red in the face. "No," she snapped. "I'm going to do this thing. I *am*!"

Lyndz and Rosie were at the bottom of the scaffolding, waiting to go up. It was Lyndz's turn next.

"Here Fliss – you can go now, if you want," Lyndz called kindly.

I pushed Fliss in front of Lyndz. I knew, just like Lyndz did, that if Fliss had to wait to go up she'd lose her bottle completely.

"Next, please!" Katya called down.

"Go on, Fliss!" we all urged her.

And Fliss began her slow climb up the scaffolding.

"What's going on?" Frankie raced over to join us. She was still breathless from her turn on the trapeze, something I'd missed because I'd been so busy with Fliss. We explained about Molly.

"But Fliss hates heights!" she gasped. "She'll never even make it up the ladder!"

We looked anxiously up the scaffolding.

"She's already up there!" Rosie gasped. "Boy, she must be mad to have climbed that far without throwing a wobbly!"

Fliss was standing on the platform, as white as a sheet. I swear we could see her trembling, even from the ground.

"It looks like she's too terrified to even hold the trapeze!" Lyndz commented.

"She'll never do it," Frankie predicted.

"Just jump down, Fliss!" I yelled. "That's the quickest way. It's dead easy."

Fliss looked down, then quickly back up again.

"Cluck, cluck, chicken!" went my stupid sister.

"SHUT UP!" the rest of us yelled together.

"I think Katya's going with her," Rosie said. "Look, they're both on the trapeze together."

As we looked up, they both pushed off from the platform. And the strange thing was that Fliss looked dead composed then. She looked all graceful and natural, just like Katya did.

"Crikey, Mischa's swinging as well!" I told the others. "Well, that's one way of getting Fliss to fall into the net, I suppose."

Mischa swung nearer and nearer until the trapezes were almost touching.

"*Now!*" shouted Katya and Mischa together.

We all held our breath. A figure fell down, down, down into the net. But it wasn't Fliss. It was *Katya*! Fliss had actually made the leap and connected with Mischa's outstretched hands – and was now swinging there with him!!

The whole ring just burst into applause. All the performers who'd been practising themselves had stopped to watch Fliss once they'd realised how terrified she was. And now everyone was buzzing with excitement.

"Don't tell me she's going to try a triple back flip now!" I grinned.

But all the excitement had obviously got to Fliss, who suddenly let go and fell into the net. One of the other trapeze artists rushed over to make sure that she was OK, and helped her down the scaffolding. All the time he was telling her how great she was. Then Katya told her how brave she'd been, and Ailsa's mum, and Ailsa's dad, and Ailsa and Bobby the clown and about a million other circus performers too. By the time she reached us again, Fliss was so pumped up with compliments I thought she was going to burst. She kept saying:

"Did you see me? Did you? I never thought I could do that! Never in a million years!"

I was pleased for her, I really was. But by the time Lyndz and Rosie had had their turns on the trapeze (and had fallen off after a couple of swings each), I was kind of sick of Fliss telling me how brilliant she was. The only good thing about it was that I could tease Molly mercilessly about it that evening.

"Yeah, well, let's see how you and your sad little friends get on with all the other circus skills, shall we?" Molly snapped nastily. "Before you get too big-headed."

The next day at the circus, we tried loads of other new skills like juggling, plate-spinning, stilt-walking and unicycling. And the following day Ailsa's dad called us all together.

"You'll find that you take to one skill more easily than the others," he told us. "So this afternoon I'd like you to start focusing on your specialist skill. It's better to perfect that rather than know how to do a little of everything. There'll be a group for each circus skill we've covered already. Feel free to try all of them again, then go back to the one where you feel most comfortable. And that won't necessarily be the one where your *friends* feel most comfortable," he concluded, staring hard at Molly and me.

"I feel most comfortable on the trapeze,"

sighed Fliss. "But I don't suppose that counts, does it? I mean, I know yesterday was just a one-off and everything, but I was obviously a natural."

The rest of us rolled our eyes,

"No Fliss, I think you'll have to pick something else," Frankie told her.

By the end of the afternoon, we'd all gone into different groups. But unfortunately I'd chosen to juggle, and so had Molly. I don't know whether it was because there were quite a few of us in that group, or whether Ailsa's dad had seen Molly and me looking daggers at each other, but he split the group into two and made sure that we were kept apart! But Lyndz was with me anyway, so that was cool.

First we started by flipping one ball up and over into each hand. Then we added another. It worked better than with doughnuts, to be honest. Then, when we felt confident with the way that felt, we added a third ball. Lyndz and I were pretty dreadful. Our balls were flipping about all over the shop. One of mine even landed on one of the plates Fliss was learning to spin in the ring behind us. That didn't go down too well, I can tell you. But then *I* didn't take too kindly to Frankie crashing into me on her unicycle.

"Watch it!" I yelled as I ended up on the floor with all my balls hitting me as they fell.

"So-rree!" sighed Frankie, picking herself up. "This isn't easy, you know!"

But, with a bit of practice, we all started getting the hang of things. We even started trying to juggle with a partner. Lyndz kept giggling because she said I was sticking my tongue out and I kept putting her off.

"I'm only concentrating," I told her.

But just at that moment I saw something which made me lose my concentration BIG time. It was Molly and Edward. They were juggling together, and they looked really good (although I hate to admit it). They'd got their timing right and everything, and they didn't drop a ball once.

"I don't believe it!" I hissed to Lyndz.

"Molly's actually *good* at something! But why does she have to be good at it in front of me?"

Before we went home, Ailsa's dad called us all together again.

"I have an important announcement to make!" he told us, grinning from ear to ear. "We're all so thrilled about how well you're doing that we want you all to perform in the circus on Saturday!"

First there was an astonished hush. Then we all started chattering at once!

"I can't do that!" squeaked Fliss. "It'll be too embarrassing!"

"Get real, it'll be brilliant!" I reassured her.

"In the first half we want you all to open the show by demonstrating the skills you've all just been practising," Ailsa's dad continued. "Then we'd like you to open the second half of the show by being those great circus favourites – yes, we want you all to be clowns! You don't have to do anything special, just run about in silly costumes and have a laugh."

How brilliant was that!

We couldn't talk about anything else all the way home. And when I did get home, Molly was already blabbing about the performance to Mum.

"It's going to be great, because me and Edward have this great routine worked out and…"

"Nanananana," I mimicked behind her back.

Molly spun round. "Will you just shut up? You're only jealous because you're so useless!"

"Oh, yeah? Well, at least I'm not all soppy and mushy over a stupid boy. I bet he's really laughing at you behind your back."

"That's it!"

Before Mum could stop her, Molly had pushed me against the fridge and was yanking at my hair. I kicked her in the shins and left her writhing on the floor.

"Stop it you two, *now*!" Mum shouted. "Just what do you think you're doing?"

She hauled us up by our ears and held us there like we were two stinky socks. "It might surprise you to learn that *I* make the decisions around here," she told us angrily. "So if I decide, in my infinite wisdom, that you're too naughty and downright unruly to even go back to the circus again, never mind to star in a performance, then my decision goes. Do you understand?"

We both grimaced and nodded.

"And remember, Kenny, that you're already on a warning after that incident at Fliss's," Mum reminded me grimly.

Molly went, "Ha ha!" behind Mum's back.

"I heard that!" Mum retorted. "There's a mound of potatoes need peeling in the kitchen, Molly, and I suggest you go and do that right now."

She shuffled off sulkily and I went upstairs. There was no way that I was going to let Molly get the better of me. And there was no way that I was going to let her upstage me in the circus performance. OK, so she was good at juggling. But if the rest of us practised hard enough, we could be pretty impressive, I felt sure. The question was, how were we ever going to practise without her seeing what we were doing?

We needed a plan. A big fat hairy plan. And I knew that it was in my head somewhere. I lay on my bed and started drifting off to sleep. And that's how it came to me. What we needed was a sleepover. And we needed to arrange one fast.

CHAPTER EIGHT

Now you'd think the others would be mega-excited at the thought of a sleepover, wouldn't you? Well, their reaction when I suggested it to them the next morning was lukewarm, to say the least.

"What's wrong with you guys?" I yelled at them. "We used to *live* for sleepovers, remember? We're the Sleepover Club!"

"We know that," said Frankie slowly. "But look what happened the last time we were together. You know, the, er, Jam Doughnut Incident. I can't exactly see our parents being overjoyed at the thought of us all getting together again."

"Well, there's no way my mum would have you lot in my house," mumbled Fliss. "And I doubt very much whether she'd let me go to a sleepover anywhere else, either."

"I reckon my mum wouldn't mind," admitted Lyndz. "But our house is still like a bomb site, so we couldn't have one there. What about your place, Kenny?"

"The whole point of us having a sleepover is to practise our routines without Molly finding out about them," I reminded her. "So there wouldn't be much point in you lot coming to my place and flaunting them under her nose, would there?"

"Mum probably would let me have a sleepover if I talked her round a bit," Frankie said. We all started grinning. I mean no-one can talk her parents round like Frankie. "Only Izzy's still poorly, so it'll have to wait," she added.

We all sighed despondently again.

Rosie was being very quiet. We all turned to her.

"Well, Rosie-Posie, it looks like you're our last hope," I put my arm round her. "What do you say?"

"I..I..I don't know," she stammered. "I mean, Mum was cool about me coming here, but I don't know whether she'd let me have a sleepover. Not when she's just got the lounge nice and everything."

"But we won't be going in the lounge," I reassured her. "All we'll be doing is rehearsing our stuff outside and sleeping in your room. Simple. She can lock the lounge door for all we care, can't she girls?"

The others nodded enthusiastically.

"Right, that's settled then," I slapped her on the back. "You work on your mum this evening and tell her that we'll be as good as gold. And tell her our reputation is at stake. Today we've got to start practising like crazy so we don't look total lame-brains on Saturday. And remember to spy on my stupid sister whenever you get the chance. I'm not having her showing us up, OK?"

We went into the Big Top to find the others all busy rehearsing. Molly started giggling with Edward Marsh as soon as she saw us.

"Ignore them," I hissed.

But it wasn't easy. Their juggling was just so darned *good*. So good, in fact, that some of the regular jugglers let them practise a few of their routines with them. Whilst Lyndz and I were struggling to keep two balls in the air, there were Molly and Edward tossing hoops about in complicated sequences and hardly making a mistake at all! Gutted!

At least Frankie, Rosie and Fliss looked pretty impressive with their skills. Frankie could ride her unicycle at speed without tumbling off it, Rosie was quite a star on stilts, and Fliss could keep four plates spinning at once with only a *teensy* amount of dithering on her part.

As we were leaving at the end of the day, Molly brushed past us.

"We're going to wipe the floor with you, suckers!" she smirked.

"Not if we've got anything to do with it!" I shouted back.

When she'd gone I turned to the others. "Now do you see why we've got to have this sleepover? I'll never live it down if she shows me up! My whole life will be cursed. Please, Rosie – you've GOT to help me."

Rosie looked at me slowly and grinned.

"Well if you put it like that," she said, "I'd better get pleading with my mum. I don't want you on my conscience for the rest of my life!"

That night I couldn't concentrate – mainly because I was wondering how Rosie was getting on, but also because Molly kept tormenting me by juggling with a load of fruit, right in front of my face.

"Pack it in!" I yelled, taking a swipe at a banana.

"Jealous, are you?" she sneered.

I would have whacked her, but the phone rang. I flew to answer it, and all I heard was Rosie yelling:

"It's on! Friday night!"

"Yippee!" I jigged about in the hall.

"But we can't pull any crazy stunts, Kenny, I mean it," warned Rosie, getting serious. "Mum says if we mess up her new lounge, we're done for. And believe me, when Mum gets mad, she gets MAD. We could even be talking about severed body parts here."

"Phew, heav-y!" I sighed. "But hey, we're not going to mess up, are we? So there's no problem."

Fortunately that's what the others said too. And by some miracle, Fliss had actually persuaded her mum to let her go to the sleepover without too much of a fight. (I put that down to hormones myself, with her being pregnant and everything. She probably didn't really know what she was saying!) We finally had a real live sleepover to look forward to! And as I said to the others, we'd be so busy perfecting our circus skills that we wouldn't even have time to *think* about getting up to any mischief. Well, that was the theory anyway.

By the time Friday night came, we were all pretty stressed out, to tell you the truth. It was obvious that Molly was MILES better than Lyndz and me at juggling. And the others weren't very confident that their own skills would be enough to take the limelight away from her.

But we still had a trump card up our sleeves. When it came to being a clown, I was the KING! Molly was about as funny as a cup of cold sick. And hopefully that would be what everyone remembered.

"OK then, let's dump our stuff and get practising!" I commanded as soon as we arrived back at Rosie's.

"But I'm hungry," moaned Rosie. "Who's for Coke and crisps first?"

"Yes!"

Anybody would think the others *wanted* Molly to make them look stupid at the circus. I was a bit disgusted that they were more bothered about their stomachs than our performance, to be honest. But I figured that I should join them, just to make sure that they didn't eat too much. So when we'd all had a snack and put our stuff in Rosie's room and got our circus equipment together to practise with, we all trooped downstairs. And who should meet us there but Tiff, Rosie's boot-faced older sister.

"Now you lot, if you set foot in the lounge, you're dead. I mean it. No-one's to go in there, understood? Spud's just finished painting the other side of the door, so we've got to leave it open so it won't stick. But just keep away from there, OK?"

We all nodded and smiled sweetly, then stuck our tongues out at her behind her back. Spud, her boyfriend, appeared and nodded hello. He never really speaks, does Spud, just nods and grunts a bit. Very strange. Anyway, he went into the kitchen to wash out his paintbrushes and we got ourselves ready to start rehearsing.

"Come on, let's go outside!" I urged the others. But when I opened the front door, I saw that it was already dropping dark and was starting to rain.

"We'll have to go to my room," Rosie said.

"But there's not enough space there now, with all our sleepover things laid out," Frankie reminded her.

"What about practising here in the hall?" I suggested. "It's big enough. We'll have plenty of room."

Rosie looked a bit uncertain.

"Come on, Rosie, we can't really do any

harm in here, can we?" said Fliss gently.

The paint was peeling from the hall skirting boards, the wallpaper was tearing off in strips and there were only bare bulbs in the sockets, no light fittings or anything.

"OK," Rosie agreed at last.

"Great!"

Fliss set up her plate-spinning stands at the far end of the hall near the kitchen. She was using special plastic plates which looked like china, but they didn't break if they fell. Frankie had plenty of space to ride up and down on her unicycle, as long as she avoided Rosie parading about on her stilts.

Lyndz and I really didn't need that much room for our juggling. Once we got into our routines, it felt pretty cool. Especially as Adam was clearly thrilled with it all. He'd wheeled himself out of the dining room so he could get a better look, and he was grinning like mad. Frankie rode over to him and started cycling backwards and forwards round him. He loved that.

"Hey, do you want to see my clown act, Adam?" I shouted, and dashed upstairs to change into my costume.

I'd been practising a routine at home, and it was about time I showed the others. I know that Ailsa's dad had said that all we needed to do was run about in silly costumes, but I wasn't going to do that. I wanted everybody to remember what a great clown I was! The others hadn't planned anything special – they just said they were going to have a laugh.

Anyway, I went into Rosie's room, pulled on the zany clown costume Mum had made for me (without Molly knowing, I hasten to add), and sprayed some shaving foam on to two paper plates.

"What are you doing with those?" squeaked Rosie as soon as I appeared downstairs again. "Please, Kenny – you promised we wouldn't make a mess!"

"Keep your knickers on!" I told her. "I'm just getting used to holding them, that's all. I'm not going to throw them, you dill!"

"Well, just make sure you don't, OK?"

Frankie was still careering about on her unicycle, picking up speed as she got used to turning in the hall.

"I'm bored with this now," Fliss moaned, removing the last plate from her pole. "Can I have a go on those moon shoes you got for your birthday, Rosie? They'll make me feel like I'm flying the way I did on the trapeze!"

We all groaned. She was *still* going on about her stunt on the trapeze, and it was driving us all crazy! Rosie told her where her moon shoes were, and carried on walking about on her stilts.

Now I don't know if you've ever seen moon shoes before. They're like boots with trampolines on their soles. So when you walk on them, you bounce up and down like an astronaut on the moon or something. And the more you bounce, the higher you go.

Well, Fliss was just in her element with those strapped to her feet.

"Look, I'm flying!" she kept yelling as she bounded down the hall.

"Just be careful in those," Frankie warned her. "We don't want any accidents, do we?"

Famous last words or what?

We were all happily doing our own thing

one minute, and the next... It still gives me goosebumps just thinking about it. And I know that we usually blame Fliss when anything goes wrong, but what happened that day was absolutely *one hundred percent* her fault, no question.

Frankie was steaming up and down the hall on her unicycle. Admittedly she was getting faster and faster, but she was always in control. That is until Miss Felicity Proudlove entered the scene. (Yup, she's Proudlove these days, ever since her mum married Andy in July. Gross, huh? Though perhaps not as bad as her old name, Sidebotham.)

"Watch me – I bet I can touch the ceiling!" she yelled.

She gave a huge bounce, somehow leapt at an angle and came crashing down right on top of Frankie.

"WAAAYHAAYY – I can't see!" Frankie shrieked, and skidded the length of the hall, the unicycle obviously out of control beneath her. Unfortunately, Rosie, who was on her stilts, could see her coming but couldn't do anything about it. One minute she was strutting about four feet in the air – the next, she'd had her stilts whipped from under her and had gone sprawling on to the ground. *CRASH!*

And this is where the really unfortunate bit comes into it.

You remember how Tiff had told us that the lounge door was open, don't you? And how under no circumstances were we to go in there? Well, we didn't have much choice. Lyndz and I were standing right by the lounge door when Rosie came hurtling towards us. Lyndz took the full force of her fall, and crashed through the door with Rosie sprawled on top of her.

The momentum of those two falling hurled me through into the lounge, which would have been OK apart from two things – a) Lyndz's juggling balls and b) my two foam pies. Somehow a ball got under my feet, and I felt like one of those clown toys trying to balance on top of it... I slithered and I staggered, and after what felt like about five whole minutes, I crashed to the floor.

All I could think of was saving myself, so I let go of the plates so that I could break my fall. I could only look on in horror as one blob of shaving foam landed slap bang in the middle of Rosie's mum's new rug, and the other slithered horribly all down one of the throws.

The words BIG and TROUBLE flashed over my eyes in neon lights.

CHAPTER NINE

For a few moments, as I lay there, there was deathly silence. Then the whole world went crazy.

"What's happened, Kenny?" shrieked Rosie, as she flew into the room. She took one look at the mess and started to wail. "Mum's going to *ki-i-ill* me!"

"It's not that bad!" I tried to sound confident as I got up and dusted myself off. "We'll soon get it cleared up. It's only shaving foam, it can't have done so much damage."

The others looked at me in disbelief.

"It's not my fault!" I told them huffily. "If Fliss

here hadn't wanted to do her moon-walking bit, none of this would have happened!"

Fliss started to protest, but was stopped by the sound of Adam's wheelchair approaching down the hall. And the sound of him laughing like a maniac.

"It is not funny, Adam!" Rosie yelled through her sobs.

"No it most certainly is NOT!" said a furious voice behind him.

Our hearts stopped. It was Tiff.

"What on EARTH is going on?" she demanded. Then she surveyed the lounge. "I *knew* something like this would happen," she raged. "I told Mum she was mad, trusting you lot here. You wreck everything you touch! Mum's going to kill you this time, Rosie, she really is!"

Rosie had somehow recovered herself, and was now staring at Tiff defiantly. "Well, she'll kill you too then, won't she? You were supposed to be supervising us, not messing about with Spud."

They stared each other down like it was the OK Corral or something. Then Tiff spoke.

"All right then, I'll help you clean it up. But if you put a foot wrong again, I'll tell Mum everything, OK?"

Rosie nodded. Then, to our total relief, Tiff went into clean-up overdrive. She gave us all instructions of where we should find various cloths and buckets of water to get the stains off the rug and the throw. She even dispatched Rosie to fetch a hairdryer so we could dry off the marks.

We were all on our hands and knees rubbing at them furiously when the front door closed.

"Mum!" screeched Tiff and Rosie together.

"Right! Everyone sit down where you are so she won't notice anything," Tiff commanded. "And act normal. That's *our* normal, Kenny, not yours!"

Charming! It wasn't my fault I was still dressed as a clown, was it?

We all flopped down. Frankie and I lay on the rug, the others sprawled over the sofa. Just at the last minute Rosie noticed the bucket of water and managed to hide it behind the door before her mum appeared.

"I thought we had a deal about no-one coming in here," she said crossly. Oh-oh, someone wasn't having a good day.

"We wanted to see your new room," Frankie smiled sweetly. "Rosie's been raving about it so much."

"And I said it would be OK if I came in with them," Tiff continued brightly. "They're hardly likely to get into any trouble if I'm here, are they?"

"I suppose not," Mrs Cartwright agreed with reluctance.

"Hey, you look tired, Mum," Tiff coaxed. "I'll make you a cup of tea if you like."

"That'd be nice, love!" Mrs Cartwright smiled. "So, how do you like the room then, girls? It's lovely, isn't it?"

"Fabulous!" we all agreed.

"Well, make sure you don't mess it up, won't you?"

Tiff ushered her mum out of the door and mouthed to us, "Start drying the stains, I'll keep Mum in the kitchen."

Once we were sure they'd gone, we all stood up.

"Yuck! I've got a wet patch on my bum!" I announced.

"Well, at least you'll have dried it off a bit," Frankie grinned. "It means we won't have to use the hairdryer so much."

"Won't your mum think it's a bit suss if she hears that whirring away?" Fliss asked.

"I've thought of that," Rosie smirked, and turned on the radio really loudly.

We took it in turns to dry the stains, and when we weren't drying we were dancing! It was great. But because we had the radio on so loud we didn't hear footsteps in the hall. We nearly jumped out of our skins when Rosie's mum suddenly reappeared.

"Just what do you think you're doing?" she demanded.

I was holding the hairdryer, and fortunately had a brainwave. I held it like a microphone and started singing at the top of my voice.

"Sorry, Mrs C," I grinned. "I just love this song, don't you?"

"You might find it sounds better if the hairdryer isn't actually *on*, Kenny," she said suspiciously. "But then again…"

She cast her eye over the throws and the rug, but thankfully the stains had gone.

"Right, I think it's time you tidied all this lot away." She looked down at all the circus props we'd abandoned on the floor. "And get yourselves ready for supper. I would appreciate a bit of quiet this evening too. I've got a mountain of work to do for college."

We picked up the stilts, juggling balls and all the other stuff, and took them upstairs. Whilst we did that, Rosie sneaked outside and emptied the bucket of water.

Before supper we had a peek in the lounge. It looked perfect. I couldn't believe that we'd actually got away with it!

But we nearly didn't, because Adam did his best to land us in it with his mum.

He's really clever, is Adam. He might not be able to speak clearly because of his cerebral palsy, but he sure knows how to manipulate people. We ended up playing stupid games with him all night, because when we said we were going to do our own stuff, he called "MUM!" and we just knew that he was going to grass on us. I mean, normally I would just love to play football games on the computer with him, but we really had more important things to be doing – like practising our routines for the circus.

When Adam finally went to bed, we looked as though we had our chance. We piled into Rosie's room, pushed all our sleeping bags and stuff to one side and started rehearsing. Rosie was making us all laugh by dancing on her stilts when Tiff burst in.

"If you lot don't shut up right now, I'm going to tell Mum!" she shouted.

"Tell me what?"

Rosie's mum was standing behind Tiff. She looked dead tired and kind of cross.

"Erm that, that... we're going to stay awake all night!" I blurted out. Well, could you have come up with anything better under the circumstances?

"Oh no you're not!" Rosie's mum raged. "In fact, you're going to get ready for bed right now, and I don't want to hear another peep out of you! And if I do, there'll be no circus performance for any of you tomorrow.

Do I make myself clear?"

Rosie certainly hadn't been kidding about how mad her mum can get!

I can't ever remember us getting ready for bed so quickly before, or so quietly. We hardly spoke to each other.

"Do you think your mum's found out about the lounge?" Frankie whispered when we were tucked up in our sleeping bags.

"She must have," Rosie replied anxiously. "I don't see why she'd be so mad otherwise. I bet Adam's told her."

We were all silent again.

"Well, you know what they say," I told the others seriously. "When the going gets tough, the tough get eating!"

"Kenny, you nutter!" The others all bashed me with their pillows.

We scrambled in our bags for our goodies and spread them out in the middle of the floor. I took three marshmallows and tried to juggle with them, but I was hopeless and kept dropping them. Soon there were sugary marks all down my pyjamas and all over my sleeping bag.

"Well, I hope you do better than that tomorrow night!" laughed Frankie. "We're going to look a right load of saddoes if that's the best we can do!"

She had a point.

I couldn't get that thought out of my head. In fact, I had a terrible nightmare. I was trying to juggle with Rosie's sofas, but I kept dropping them. Then Molly picked me up and started tossing me to Edward Marsh. Fliss and Frankie kept flying past me on a trapeze, but couldn't reach me. And Lyndz was wheeling Adam about and they were both laughing crazily. It was horrible, just horrible.

It was quite a relief to wake up the next morning, to be honest. But then it hit home. Today was the day that we were going to be performing in front of loads of people – *and we hadn't practised enough*!

At least we had a session at the circus in the morning to try to sort ourselves out. But that didn't start well. Molly was already rehearsing with Edward Marsh and two of the circus jugglers when we got there.

I couldn't bear to watch.

"Hey, your sister's really good!" Ailsa gushed enthusiastically as soon as she saw us. "Have you been practising together?"

"No way!" I told her scornfully.

"Oh," she shrugged. "Well, let's see what you can do, then."

Lyndz and I took out our juggling balls and started throwing them to each other. Or at least we tried to. More went on the floor than anywhere else.

There was a load of slow clapping behind us. My stupid sister!

"Well, you're going to really wow them with that display, aren't you!" she jeered. "You might as well give up now and leave it to the professionals!"

She turned back and started one of her intricate routines with Edward Marsh. But then, saviours of the hour, the Circus Jamboree jugglers came over.

"It's only your timing that's a bit off," one of them smiled. "Look, keep your eyes on the balls and concentrate. That's all there is to it."

They encouraged us to start juggling slowly. Then, when we'd got our confidence, they started juggling with us, throwing balls to us and receiving ours. After almost an hour we'd really got it together, and I felt *grrrreat!*

"Thanks, guys!"

"No problem!" they grinned. "You're going to be fantastic this evening. Just forget about the audience."

Whilst we'd been brushing up our juggling skills, the others had also been having extra tuition, so by the end of the morning we were full of beans and raring to go for the evening's performance.

"Shouldn't we practise a clown routine?" asked Fliss anxiously. "I know Ailsa's dad said we didn't have to, but we don't want to look stupid, do we?"

"Look, Fliss," I said, putting my arm round her. "The only person who's going to look stupid is Molly. I've got a few tricks up my sleeve for the clown part. All you've got to do is follow my lead!"

"Are you sure you know what you're

doing?" asked Rosie. "It's your plans that usually get us into trouble."

"Look, do you want to humiliate Molly or not?" I demanded.

We looked over to where Molly was grinning and mouthing "Losers" to us.

"I guess so!" the others agreed.

"Well, that's settled then," I told them. "Just leave it to me, and meet me here half an hour before the show starts. I'll fill you in on what you have to do then."

As soon as I got home, I shut myself in my bedroom. I put on my clown suit and went through all my routines. Then I worked out how I could get Molly once and for all.

By the time I got to the circus for the evening performance, I was really pumped up. But the others seemed kind of nervous.

"We're going to have a blast!" I assured them. "And this is what you need to know for our clown section…"

I got them all in a huddle and whispered the most important information to them. I'd brought a prop bag with me and I showed them what was inside.

"Right you lot, curtain's up in five minutes. Are you ready?" Ailsa's dad called as he rushed past.

The other performers were doing their warm-up exercises. I could see Molly messing about with Edward Marsh, laughing and stuff.

"Well, you won't be laughing when *I've* finished with you!" I grinned to myself.

And I grabbed my juggling balls and started to practise.

"Welcome, ladies and gentlemen, to Circus Jamboree!" Ailsa's dad was already introducing us. "We are proud to present – our young circus students!"

There was a blast of music, and the performers were pushing us out into the ring. This was it! There was no going back now!

We ran out. I couldn't BELIEVE how many people there were. I couldn't pick out any faces because only the ring itself was lit up, but you could tell that the Big Top was *packed*.

I took up my position, threw my balls into the air and – something cannoned into me, making me drop them all on the ground. The crowd started to roar with laughter. That certainly wasn't part of the plan. What was going on?

CHAPTER TEN

Dazed, I turned to see Molly grinning at me.

"Sorry, sis!" she smirked as she weaved her way across the ring, juggling her balls rhythmically with Edward Marsh.

"OK Kenny, keep cool!" I told myself.

I'd just got into my stride with my own juggling when there was a crash over on the other side of the ring. I stopped in my tracks to see Frankie scrambling up from the floor with her unicycle on top of her.

"Molly walked into her on purpose," Lyndz whispered to me. "I saw her."

Man, this was too much! I was getting so mad that steam was coming out of my ears.

"She's not going to get away with this!" I hissed.

But looking across at Molly, it seemed like butter wouldn't melt in her mouth. She was doing all these intricate routines, and they all seemed to involve making me and my mates look as stupid as possible. Like when they juggled right into Fliss's spinning plates.

"Over to you!" they kept yelling, and *crash*! One of their balls would knock one of Fliss's plates off its pole on to the ground.

"Hey, watch it!" Fliss squeaked. She was so shocked that she forgot to keep spinning the other plates. And as soon as she remembered, Molly and her stupid sidekick juggled another of their balls into them anyway. Soon, all poor Fliss's plates were lying on the ground and Fliss was nearly in tears.

"You were never much good at things like this, were you Fliss!" Molly smirked as Fliss scrambled to pick her plates up. "And that trapeze act was just a fluke, too!"

"It was not!" Fliss spat angrily, and looked up just in time to see Molly walk right into the path of Rosie on her stilts.

"No..no..NO!" Rosie yelled as she came crashing to the ground – right on top of Lyndz!

"*Look out!*" screamed Lyndz, dropping her juggling balls. But it was too late. Frankie had already run into Rosie and toppled off her unicycle again. And although I'd seen it all happening, it was almost like I was watching it on a film and couldn't do anything about it.

"Move, Kenny! NOW!" Frankie screamed at me – but it was no good. With a thud, I landed on the ground on top of her.

"Right, you've got it coming, Molly!" I yelled, and made to storm over to her. But just at that moment, the lights dimmed and we were being ushered out of the ring by Ailsa's dad and the other performers.

"Weren't they wonderful!" Ailsa's dad roared to the audience. "Let's give them a big hand! And don't worry – we'll be seeing more of our students later in the performance!"

It was like he hadn't even *noticed* what Molly had been doing!

"You two were fantastic!" I heard Simon, one of the jugglers, congratulating Molly and Edward. "You could get a job with us any day!"

That was too much to bear, it really was. The last straw, the final frontier, the END.

"We've *got* to make sure we sort out Molly and her stupid little friend next time!" I snarled at the others.

"You're not kidding!" moaned Frankie. "My bum's black and blue, she knocked me over so many times."

"And did you see what your two-faced sister did to my plates?" wailed Fliss. "It was horrible the way the audience kept laughing as though it was part of the act!"

"Well, Molly will be laughing on the other side of BOTH her faces when the audience see our clown act!" I assured them bravely. "Let's all get changed so we can sort everything out."

We went into the smaller tent next to the Big Top which served as a dressing room. We'd left our costumes in there earlier, along with my prop bag.

"What if Molly sees us?" asked Lyndz.

"I wouldn't worry about that," Frankie said. "She was too busy lapping up praise last time I saw her."

We peeped out of the tent, and could just see Molly giggling and joking with some of the other performers.

"Told you!" Frankie said with a sigh.

By the time we were all changed, the tent was empty because all the other performers were involved in the show. I tossed my secret props to the others and we got to work. I'd brought cans of shaving foam and paper plates. I'd also got one of those fake flowers filled with water, and loads of cans of custard which we emptied into two big bowls.

"How are we going to hide all this lot, then?" Rosie asked.

"We'll just keep it in here until the start of the second half," I told her. "Then, whilst I'm doing all my funny stuff, all you've got to do is run on with everything and mess about with it a bit. You know, pretend you're going to throw it into the audience and stuff. But make sure you watch me for my cue!"

The others all nodded nervously.

There was a burst of applause from the Big Top.

"It sounds like the first half's finished!" I said. "It won't be long now…"

We all hung around because we didn't want to leave our things unattended and risk Molly discovering them. Then Ailsa rushed over to us. She was in a green spangly costume and was looking flushed after her acrobatic display.

"Hey, you did well," she grinned. "It's a pity your sister spoilt it, though."

"Don't worry, it's pay-back time now!" I told her grimly.

She looked puzzled. "What are you going to do?"

"Oh, you'll see. There isn't any water around here, is there?" I asked.

"For a drink, you mean?" she asked.

"No, in a bucket or something."

"Well, there are fire buckets standing by all the exits, just in case," she explained. "But it's kind of dangerous to use water in the ring, in case the other performers slip and hurt themselves. You're not going to do anything stupid, are you?"

"No, 'course not," I assured her, my fingers crossed behind my back. "I just want to be prepared."

Molly brushed past us.

"Well, that was a pathetic display, I must say," she smarmed. "I don't think anyone will be inviting *you* to join the circus, will they?"

We pulled gruesome faces at her, but she just laughed. When she'd gone, Rosie said, "I hope your plan works, Kenny, because I'm really SICK of your sister."

We all had to agree with that.

Suddenly Ailsa's dad appeared.

"Are you ready for your clown acts?" he smiled. "It'll only be for a few moments, so just go out there and enjoy it."

Then he ran into the Big Top and announced:

"Now, ladies and gentlemen, the moment you've all been waiting for! Tonight we have some very special clowns for you. Put your hands together for… our students!"

Loud clown-type music started blaring out.

"Have you got your props?" I asked the others quickly . "Just remember, we've got to humiliate Molly – TO THE MAX!"

We all ran out into the ring. Then, one minute I was on my feet – the next I was making my entrance skidding across the sawdust on my front.

"What the…?" I looked up, dazed.

"Enjoy your trip, sucker?" laughed Molly. She'd only stuck out her leg to make me fall over hadn't she, the creep!

By the time I'd limped over to the others, they were all pretending to throw the foam pies at the audience, then pulling away at the last minute. When Molly got closer to us, I went up behind her and tapped her on the shoulder. She turned round – and I twanged my braces in her face.

"Take that, dog breath!" I grinned.

That was the cue! Suddenly the whole Sleepover Club crowded round Molly so that she was cut off from her little friend Edward Marsh.

"Let me go, you creeps!" she said through gritted teeth.

"Not likely!" I beamed. "You know what the clowns taught us. You've got to interact with other people, remember?"

I poked my plastic flower right in Molly's face, but she was a bit too quick for that. She ducked and I ended up squirting Fliss in the eye.

"GidoutofitKenny!" Fliss squeaked, trying to wipe her eyes and at the same time hang on to the plate she was holding.

"I'm going to show you what *real* clowning is all about, creeps!" Molly spat, and looked round for Edward Marsh.

Catching her off guard, Frankie got her right in the chops with a foam pie. SPLAT!

"You morons!" Molly spluttered, wiping the foam flecks away.

"Oh, morons, are we?" Fliss asked menacingly – and whammed Molly with a second pie. THWACK!

I poured a bowl of custard down the front of her trousers as well. And all the while, the audience was in complete hysterics.

"Do you think she needs some water to wash her down?" I called out to them, running to one of the exits for a water bucket. "Should I throw this at her?"

The kids in the audience were going crazy! "YESSS!" they were screaming.

I ran back towards Molly – but suddenly the bucket was whipped out of my hands. Molly had wrenched it from my grasp.

"Gimme that, scuzz brain!" she snarled, and swung the bucket back.

"Don't do it, Molly! it was only a jo—"

We ducked down just before she threw the whole lot over the audience. And it wasn't just *any* part of the audience, either.

"Mrs Weaver... Mrs Poole!"

Frankie went white as she recognised our teacher and headmistress. Their hair was plastered to their faces and their make-up was starting to run. This had turned into a disaster of earth-shattering proportions!!

Ailsa's dad rushed on, blew his whistle and ushered us all from the ring. The rest of the audience were still shrieking and clapping. Then suddenly, I heard a voice that

I knew all too well...

"You little *idiots*!" roared Dad, grabbing me and Molly. "You've gone way too far this time!"

What a way for the show to end!

When me and Molly got home, we were subjected to an hour's lecture on behaving responsibly in public and how we had let everybody down. Wah, wah, wah. I had the most miserable weekend *ever*. And when I saw the others on the following Monday at school, it seemed that they had endured similar tortures. And Mrs Weaver gave us loads of extra homework, although she didn't mention anything about Saturday night.

Molly grovelled and apologised to Mrs Weaver and Mrs Poole straight after school, under Mum's beady eye. Then Mum accompanied us all to the circus, where we had to make a formal apology to Ailsa's dad.

"If there's anything we can do to make it up to you..." Frankie said.

"That won't be necessary," Ailsa's dad

said, trying to look serious. "But what you lot did could have had serious consequences, you know."

As we were leaving, Bobby the clown winked at us. "Hey, I'm going to have to watch out for you lot taking my job!" he grinned. "I've been waiting all my life for a laugh like you got the other night!"

After that, it was kind of like living in a minefield in our house. I had to be on my best behaviour *all the time.* It was a nightmare. And even when I hadn't even done anything wrong, I got bawled out by Mum and Dad anyway. They said they were still humiliated by me and Molly showing them up in public like that. But I guess things are getting a bit calmer at last.

We're all going to a secret meeting now, to suss out how we can persuade our parents to let us have another sleepover before we turn into Old Age Pensioners! Well, as they say in the circus, the show must go on...